This Topsy and Tim book belongs to

_____

Topsy and Tim
Go on a Train

By Jean and Gareth Adamson

Illustrations by Belinda Worsley

A catalogue record for this book is available from the British Library

Published by Ladybird Books Ltd
A Penguin Company
Penguin Books Ltd., 80 Strand, London WC2R 0RL, UK
Penguin Books Australia Ltd., 707 Collins Street, Melbourne, Victoria 3008, Australia
Penguin Group (NZ) 67 Apollo Drive, Rosedale, North Shore 0632, New Zealand

004

ISBN: 978-1-40930-424-1
Printed in China

www.topsyandtim.com

Topsy and Tim were going to visit their granny.
They were going by train because Granny lived
a long way away.
"Hurry up, Topsy and Tim," said
Mummy. "We mustn't miss our train."

They were taking lots of luggage with them, so Mummy
called a taxi to drive them to the station.

"I wish we could go faster," said Tim. "We'll miss the train."

"No we won't," said Mummy.

They reached the station with plenty of time
to spare.

The kind taxi driver found a special trolley for their bags. Topsy and Tim helped push it through the booking hall.

People were queuing to buy tickets at the ticket office. "I'm glad I came to buy our tickets yesterday," said Mummy. "Now we don't have to join that queue."

"Our train leaves from platform two," said Mummy.
She showed their tickets to the platform guard.
"Platform two is over the bridge," he told them.

"Phew!" said Tim, as they pushed
their trolley up the slope to the bridge.
"Wheee!" said Topsy, as they
trundled it down the other side.

There was a little shop on the platform. Topsy and
Tim chose some comics to look at on the journey.

A lot of people were waiting for the train. At last a loudspeaker told them that it had arrived.

"Here's our train," shouted Topsy.
"I saw it first," said Tim. It was quite
a scramble to get on to the train.

"Stay close to me and mind the gap between the
train and the platform," said Mummy.

There was a squash inside the train too,
but clever Mummy found some empty seats.
"I want to sit by the window," said Tim.

"It's not fair," said Topsy. "I want to sit by the window."
Luckily, there were two empty window seats, so everyone
was happy.

A whistle blew and the train began to move.
"We're off," said Mummy.
"Hooray!" shouted Topsy and Tim.

Soon the train was rushing through the countryside.
Topsy and Tim looked out of the window to see
what they could spot.

"I can see a pony," said Topsy.

"I can see some cows," said Tim.

"Tickets, please," said a friendly voice. It was the ticket inspector. He had come to check their tickets.
"Are you off on your holidays?" he asked.
"We're going to stay with our granny," said Topsy.

"Can I come, too?" asked the ticket inspector, but he was only joking.

"Are we nearly there?" asked Tim.

"Not yet," said Mummy.

The door at the end of the carriage opened and a lady pushed a rattling trolley towards them. It was filled with things to eat and drink.

"Would you both like a sandwich?" asked Mummy.
"I want a ham sandwich," said Tim.
"A cheese sandwich, please," said Topsy.
They both had some orange juice and Mummy had
a cup of coffee.

It made the carriage look gloomy and strange.

"Oooer!" said Topsy.

"My ears feel funny," said Tim.

"Drink some orange juice," said Mummy. "Then they'll feel better."

At last the train stopped at Granny's station.
"There's Granny!" shouted Topsy and Tim.
They both wanted to hold Granny's hand.
"I'm glad I've got two hands," laughed Granny.
"I wish I had three!" said Mummy.

Now turn the page and help
Topsy and Tim solve a puzzle.

Topsy and Tim are helping Mummy with the trolley. Look closely at the picture below. Then look at the pictures opposite. Can you work out which one is exactly the same?

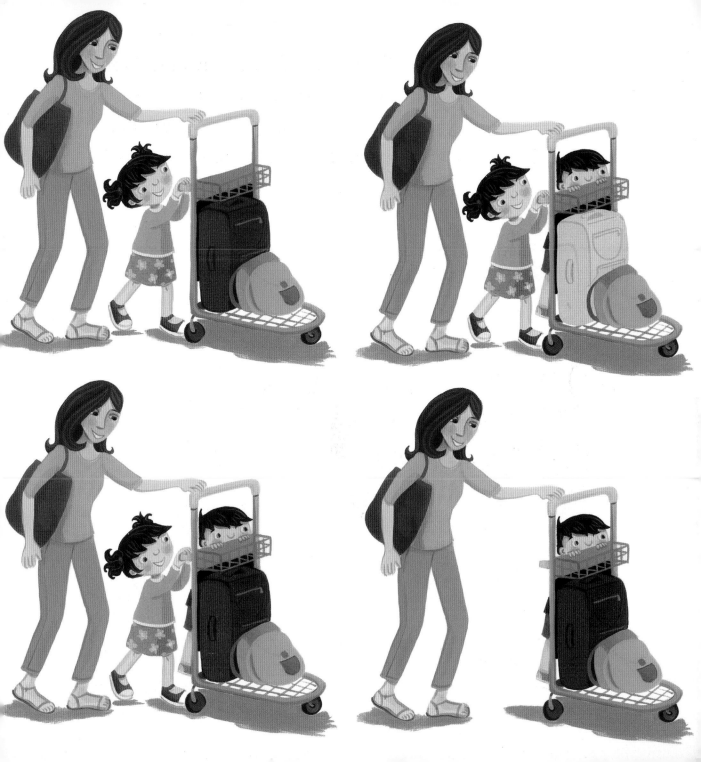

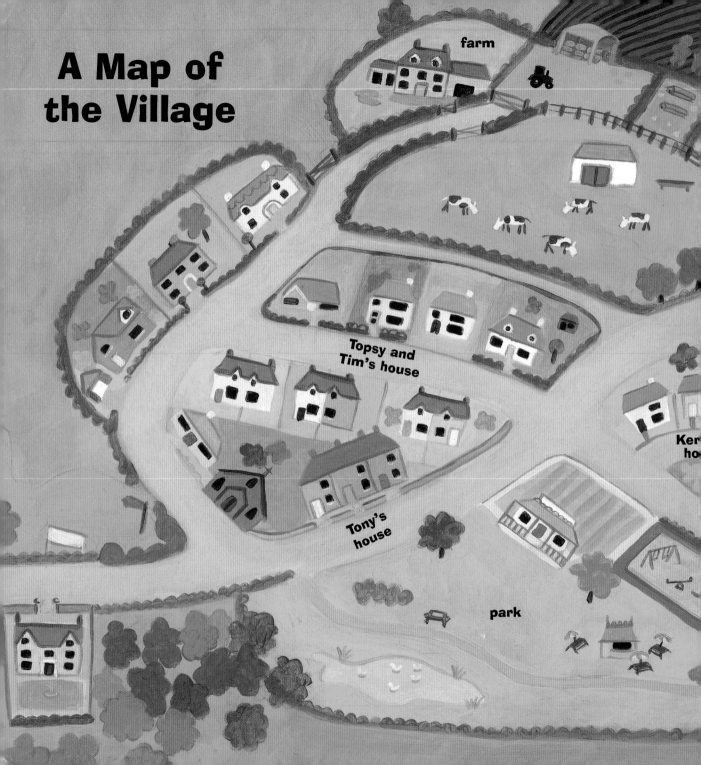

A Map of the Village

farm

Topsy and
Tim's house

Ker
ho

Tony's
house

park

garage

health
centre

post
office

church

primary school

nursery school

police station

Have you read all the Topsy and Tim stories?

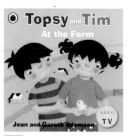 **Topsy and Tim — At the Farm**
☐ 9781409303367

 **Topsy and Tim — Go Camping**
☐ 9781409303336

 **Topsy and Tim — Go on an Aeroplane**
☐ 9781409300571

 **Topsy and Tim — Go on a Train**
☑ 9781409304241

 **Topsy and Tim — Go to Hospital**
☐ 9781409304234

 **Topsy and Tim — Start School**
☐ 9781409300830

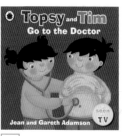 **Topsy and Tim — Go to the Doctor**
☐ 9781409303343

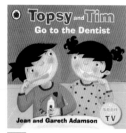 **Topsy and Tim — Go to the Dentist**
☐ 9781409300588

 **Topsy and Tim — Have a Birthday Party**
☐ 9781409300618

 **Topsy and Tim — Meet Father Christmas**
☐ 9781409311591

 **Topsy and Tim — Meet the Police**
☐ 9781409308836

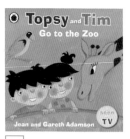 **Topsy and Tim — Go to the Zoo**
☐ 9781409300847

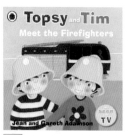 **Topsy and Tim — Meet the Firefighters**
☐ 9781409307211

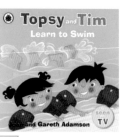 **Topsy and Tim — Learn to Swim**
☐ 9781409300601

 **Topsy and Tim — Play Football**
☐ 9781409303350

 **Topsy and Tim — Safety First**
☐ 9781409308829

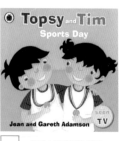 **Topsy and Tim — Sports Day**
☐ 9781409309468

 **Topsy and Tim — Have Itchy Heads**
☐ 9781409307204

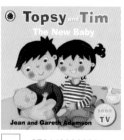 **Topsy and Tim — The New Baby**
☐ 9781409300564

 **Topsy and Tim — Visit London**
☐ 9781409309475

All stories by Jean and Gareth Adamson.

 Available on the App Store

The Topsy and Tim app is available for iPad, iPhone and iPod touch.

It is also available on Android devices.